MEET THE AUTHOR – NARINDER DHAMI

What is your favourite animal?
Cats – I have five of them
What is your favourite boy's name?
Freddie
What is your favourite girl's name?
Natasha
What is your favourite food?
Curry, especially my mum's
What is your favourite music?
1970s' punk and bhangra
What is your favourite hobby?
Watching football (I support
Wolves)

MEET THE ILLUSTRATOR – MIKE PHILLIPS

What is your favourite animal?
Dog
What is your favourite boy's name?
Ben (my son's name)
What is your favourite girl's name?
Hannah and Olivia (my daughters)
What is your favourite food?
Cheese
What is your favourite music?
Anything that makes my feet tap
What is your favourite hobby?
Armchair cricket supporting

Contents

Chapter 1
An Idiot!

Do you know what I am?

I'm a total idiot!

That's right.

I'm an idiot. A fool. A mug. A total loser.

I'm all of those things.

Right now I could be sitting in the sun in Florida with my mum.

But I'm not.

I'm here in my bedroom, and Dad's yelling at me like he always does.

"Robbie! Have you cleaned up your bedroom yet? ROBBIE!"

Dad was calling me from downstairs. He was getting mad, I could tell. Well, so what? Dad was always mad these days. He'd win first prize in a Mad Dad contest, no problem!

I pressed the button on my computer and watched the screen spring into life. Have you ever felt really fed up with your family? Have you ever wished you could just get rid of them, and start all over again with a new lot? I felt like that about my dad. I wish there was a Dad Swap Shop. I'd take him down there and change him for a new model.

Dad was looking for a fight with me. I could hear him running up the stairs, *thump, thump, thump*, like a baby elephant. Now he was at the top. I counted his footsteps along the landing. One, two, three, four – *BANG!*

My bedroom door crashed open.

"Robbie, I'm talking to you!" Dad shouted. He was very angry. "Have you cleaned up your bedroom yet?"

I didn't say anything. I didn't have to. I hadn't made my bed, my school uniform lay on the floor and there were CDs everywhere. So now Dad and I were going to have a big fight. We'd already had a million fights this week.

"You *haven't* cleaned up!" Dad yelled. "How many times do I have to tell you?"

"I'll do it later," I mumbled, but I kept on looking at my computer screen. I wanted to check my e-mails and see if Mum had replied to my last message.

"That's what you always say," Dad moaned. He rushed into the room and tripped over my sports bag. I clapped my hand over my mouth, trying not to laugh.

"You spend too much time on that computer," Dad snapped, kicking at a dirty sock. "Get this room cleaned up, Robbie. Right now."

"Later." I swung round in my chair. I glared at Dad. We were like two boxers in a ring.

"*Now*," Dad repeated firmly.

We stared at each other long and hard. One of us would have to give in, and it wasn't going to be me.

Right at that moment the doorbell rang. Dad turned away with a sigh. I slid out of my chair, and ran downstairs to see who it was.

Saved by the bell, I thought.

Dad's been like this ever since Mum left. He used to be fun, but now he's a pain in the neck. He's hardly ever at home because he's always doing overtime at work. We never do stuff together any more. He nags me all the time. *Robbie, clean up your bedroom. Robbie, do your homework. Robbie, do this. Robbie, do that.*

I wish I'd gone to America with Mum and her new boyfriend.

When Mum and Dad split up, they said it was up to me where I wanted to live. I could go to Florida with Mum and Scott, or stay here with Dad.

Now you know why I'm an idiot.

I said I'd stay with Dad. I didn't like to think of him all alone, and I knew he didn't want me to go. Big mistake. All Dad wanted was someone to shout at. And I'm getting sick of it.

I pulled open the front door. My best mate Joe stood outside.

SORRY!

Let's go back a bit.

Joe *used* to be my best mate, but right now I don't want to hang out with him any more. He just gets right up my nose, like everything else these days.

"Hi, Robbie," Joe mumbled. He stared down at his feet, looking awkward. "Um – me and some of the lads are going to the park to play footy."

Joe and I have had about a million arguments this week, too. We had a big fight at school yesterday, and Joe said I had a bad attitude. Can you believe that? Just because I was moaning about Dad. And you know what else Joe said? He said I should give Dad a break!

Yeah, right. When was Dad going to give *me* a break? I missed Mum, and I was tired of being nagged all the time.

Joe and I stared at each other.

"Well?" Joe said at last. "Do you want to come or not?"

What I really wanted to say was "Yes". But I didn't.

"No, thanks," I said with a yawn.

Joe looked hurt, which made me feel a bit guilty. "I suppose you're going out with your *new* mates," he muttered.

I frowned. "What new mates?"

"Crusher Capstick and his gang," said Joe. "I saw you hanging around with them after school yesterday."

Crusher Capstick was in our class at school. He was a pain and a bully and a pest, and all the teachers hated him. Most of the kids did, too. Crusher was always in trouble for starting fights or talking back at the teachers or bunking off school. But he was a laugh, and he didn't care about anything or anyone. I wanted to be that way, too.

"It's none of your business," I said, and slammed the door in Joe's face.

Nice one, Robbie! Now my dad *and* my best friend hated me.

My life was a mess.

And it could only get worse.

What do *you* think I should do? Should I stay here with Dad, or should I go to Florida? I don't know any more.

I sat at the bottom of the stairs, and thought for a bit. Then I made up my mind. I'd e-mail Mum and ask her to send me a ticket to America. I'd move in with her and Scott, and everything would be cool.

I didn't care if I never saw Dad again. Or Joe.

Dad wouldn't miss me anyway. He was at work most of the time. And if he wanted to nag someone, he could get a dog!

I ran upstairs. I'd e-mail my mum right now, and by next week, I'd be gone. I felt a pain deep down inside me, but I stopped thinking about it. I knew it was for the best.

Dad had gone into his bedroom and shut the door. I was glad. I didn't want to tell him I was leaving until it was all sorted out.

I sat down and clicked on my e-mails.

I hope Mum lets me bring the computer, I thought. My computer was the best friend

I had right now. I wasn't going to leave it behind.

I only had one new e-mail, and it wasn't from Mum. It was boring junk mail. But for once, this one looked interesting.

Is your life a mess?

Do you think it can only get worse?

WE CAN HELP!

Chapter 2
Kaboom!

I never open junk mail. Dad always tells me to delete it, in case it's got a virus.

But this time I didn't press delete. I just sat and stared at the message on my screen.

Is your life a mess?

Do you think it can only get worse?

The words bounced through my brain. They were the same words I'd said to myself just now. The very same words. So what? It didn't mean anything. But it *was* strange.

WE CAN HELP!

I looked at the *Delete* key, but I didn't touch it. Instead, I moved my mouse, and clicked on the e-mail so I could read it all.

KABOOM!

I got the fright of my life. A shower of silver stars exploded in front of me. The stars began to rain softly down from the top of the screen to the bottom. The silver light was so bright, it seemed as if the stars were floating right off the screen and around the room. I blinked.

Is your life a mess?

The words were swirling and fizzing around on the screen in front of me. They were moving so fast, I was beginning to feel a bit dizzy.

Do you think it can only get worse?

Pink and blue rockets were shooting around the screen like fireworks. Now I really did feel dizzy. I was so dazzled by the bright colours, I could only just make out the next words.

We can help.

But be careful what you wish for.

You might just get it!

Someone tapped me on the shoulder.

"OH!" I gasped, spinning round.

I hadn't heard Dad come into the room. I was so shocked, my finger slipped on the mouse and the message vanished. I didn't mean to do it, but it was better that way. I didn't want Dad to see that I'd been looking at junk mail.

Dad frowned at me. "Were you looking at junk mail?" he asked crossly.

"No," I mumbled.

"What have I told you?" Dad snapped. "You should always delete junk mail in case it's a virus—"

"I know," I cut in. "Will you stop nagging me?"

"I only nag because you don't do what you're told," Dad grumbled. "Look at this mess." He waved his hand at the room. "I've asked you to clean this up a hundred times."

"I'll do it when I'm ready," I muttered. "I've got other things on my mind."

"Like what?" asked Dad.

He bent down and picked up my crumpled school shirt.

"You don't know how lucky you are, Robbie," he said, sitting on my bed. He wasn't really talking to me. It was as if he was talking to himself. "I wish I was 11 years old like you, with no problems or worries."

"Oh yeah?" I shouted.

I was very angry. Dad never listened to me. Never. Did he think my life was really that great?

"Well, I wish you were the same age as me, too," I yelled at him. "Then you'd see that I've got LOADS of problems!"

Be careful what you wish for.

You might just get it!

Chapter 3
All Change

There wasn't a flash of silver light. There wasn't a puff of glittering smoke. Just for a few seconds, I felt a bit dizzy again. That was all.

But in those few seconds, something had happened. Something *huge*.

At first I thought I was seeing things. I blinked. Once. Twice. Three times. But I wasn't seeing things. It was real.

Dad was still sitting on my bed. He still had my school shirt in his hand. But he wasn't Dad.

He'd shrunk. Now he was smaller than I was. His shirt and tie were hanging off him. He looked like a kid wearing his dad's clothes. His hair was weird, too. He always wore it short and cropped, but now it was longer and messy, just like mine. He had freckles on his nose. Just like mine.

I gasped, my eyes wide open in shock.

Dad looked just like he did in the old photos we kept in the loft.

Dad looked *11 years old.*

"What's happened to me?" Dad asked in a high voice. "I feel funny."

He grabbed his throat. "What's happened to my voice?" he squeaked. "I *sound* funny!"

I stared at him. I didn't know what to say.

"You'd better look in the mirror," I said at last.

Dad stood up and peered into the mirror. He jumped back when he saw himself.

"Is this some kind of trick mirror, Robbie?" he demanded.

I gave a sigh. I might have known Dad would blame me for this weird thing that had happened to him! Then, suddenly, I remembered the e-mail.

Be careful what you wish for.

You might just get it!

"Robbie!" Dad was starting to sound very nervous. "Is this a joke?"

"No," I said. "You've shrunk. Look at your clothes. They're too big for you."

Dad stared down at himself. His eyes were almost popping out of his head.

"What's going on?" he gasped.

"I think you're 11 years old," I told him.

Dad looked at me as if I was mad.

"You wanted to be 11," I said. "And now you are."

"Don't be silly," Dad began. Then he stopped and peered in the mirror again. He looked at himself this way and that. He closed his eyes and opened them again.

"Oh no!" he groaned at last. "I *am* 11 years old!" He sat down on my bed and put his head in his hands. "I'm ill! There's something very wrong with me!"

"I don't think so," I said. I couldn't see how opening the junk e-mail had done this. I didn't believe in magic. Wishes and wizards and spells were for kids.

But something strange had happened.

Dad jumped up from the bed and tripped over his long jeans.

"I'd better go to the doctor's right away," he said. He sounded upset.

"It's Saturday," I reminded him. "They're closed."

"We'll go to the hospital then," Dad mumbled. He still looked very shocked. "You'll have to lend me some of your clothes, Robbie. I can't go like this."

I gave Dad a pair of my jeans, a T-shirt and some trainers.

"I don't know why you're getting so worked up," I said. "You wanted to be 11 years old again, didn't you?"

"Don't be cheeky, Robbie," he snapped. "I'm still your dad."

"But you're only 11!" I said, with a grin. "And you're smaller than I am!"

Dad looked at me angrily, and hurried out of the room. I went after him. Before I left, I glanced over at my computer. Maybe I should have another look at that e-mail. Maybe it would help Dad get back to normal.

"Don't be stupid," I told myself, as I went downstairs. "You don't believe in magic!"

Dad was in the hall, staring at himself in the mirror. He had the car keys in his hand.

"Dad!" I started to laugh. "You can't drive to the hospital!"

Dad looked cross. "Why not?" he asked.

"Because you're 11!" I could hardly get the words out because I was chuckling so much.

"I only *look* 11," Dad replied. "Inside I'm still 32. And it's miles to the hospital. We're going by car."

"I don't think this is a good idea," I told him, as he shut the front door.

Our silver car was parked at the side of the road. Dad walked over and unlocked it.

"Just get in, Robbie," he said, and slid into the driver's seat.

I climbed in next to him. But I couldn't stop myself grinning when I saw that Dad's feet didn't even reach the pedals!

Dad turned red. "I'll just move the seat forward," he muttered.

He was moving the seat when there was a tap at the window. We both looked up.

A policeman was staring in at us.

"I told you this wasn't a good idea," I whispered.

Dad wound the window down, trying to look cool.

"Hello, officer," he said.

The policeman didn't look very friendly. "And what are you two kids up to?" he asked. You could see he didn't trust us, not one bit.

"Well—" Dad began.

I elbowed him in the ribs.

"Ow!" moaned Dad.

"Me and my brother are just getting something for my dad," I said quickly. I reached under the seat and pulled out a map. "We're going back inside now."

"But—" Dad began again.

"Stop arguing," I said. "Or I'll tell Dad, and then you'll really be in trouble!"

"That isn't funny, Robbie," Dad whispered, but he got out of the car all the same.

We went back to the house. The policeman stood and watched us the whole time. He only walked off when we'd gone inside and shut the door.

"Do you still think it's a good idea to take the car?" I asked.

"Maybe not," Dad mumbled. He had gone a bit red. "We'll walk into town and get the bus."

We set off again. I have to tell you, it was really weird having a dad the same age as me. The worst thing was, Dad still kept on nagging me. "Robbie, do up your shoelaces. Robbie, mind that lady with the baby buggy. Robbie, don't run across the road." It was doing my head in getting told off by someone who was the same age as me!

We were walking down Turtle Street when Dad stopped.

"Oh no!" he gasped.

"What?"

"There." Dad pointed down the road. "It's my boss, Mr Green!"

I looked where he was pointing. Mr Green was heading straight towards us.

"Quick!" Dad grabbed my arm. "We've got to hide. I can't let him see me like this!"

"Don't worry," I whispered. "He won't know who you are."

"I suppose you're right," Dad agreed, but he still looked worried.

Mr Green had seen us, and was smiling at me. I'd met him a few times before. He seemed OK, but Dad said he was a slave-driver in the office. He told me it was Mr Green's fault that he had to work so hard, and do so much overtime.

"Hello, Robbie," called Mr Green. "Nice to see you again." His eyes moved to Dad. "And who's this?"

"This is my cousin," I said.

At just that moment, Dad said, "I'm one of his mates."

Mr Green looked confused while Dad and I glared at each other. "Well, it's nice to meet you anyway," he said. "And how's your dad, Robbie?"

"He's not too bad," I replied. "He's just not feeling himself at the moment."

I thought that was quite funny, but Dad shot me a very annoyed look.

Mr Green nodded. "Yes, your dad's working too hard," he said. "I keep telling him to slow down a bit, but he says he's fine."

My mouth fell open in shock. That wasn't what Dad had said to *me*.

"Tell him from me to take it easy." Mr Green waved at us and went on his way. "See you later."

I turned round slowly to stare at Dad. He was bright red, and kicking a stone along the gutter.

"What's going on, Dad?" I asked. "You said you *had* to spend so much time at the office."

"Well ..." Dad mumbled. "The thing is, I've been worried about money. We haven't got the money from your mum's job now. That's why I've been doing so much overtime."

For a moment I felt angry with myself. I should have guessed we didn't have so much money now. But then I felt really angry with Dad, too.

"Why didn't you tell me?" I wanted to know.

"Because it's up to me to sort it out," said Dad.

"You didn't have to lie to me. I'm not a kid!"

"Yes, you are," Dad said.

"Well, so are you!" I yelled. "So there!"

And we stood face to face, glaring at each other.

Chapter 4
Crusher

Dad looked really angry. I didn't know what he was going to do next. But then we heard a shout behind us.

"Robbie! Hey, Robbie!"

I looked round. Crusher Capstick and his gang were coming down the street towards us. Crusher was striding along in front of the others. He had his baseball cap on back to front, and he looked pretty cool.

I raised my hand. "Hey, Crusher," I called back. "How's it going?"

"Crusher?" Dad frowned. "What kind of a name is that?"

I took no notice. Crusher and the others stopped in front of us, and looked Dad up and down.

"Who's your geeky mate, Robbie?" Crusher asked with a grin. The rest of the gang, Ed Willis, Rocky Stone and Kirk Bunn, all laughed.

"This is my—" I stopped myself. I had almost said *Dad*. "This is Terry."

"Mr Carter to you," Dad said coldly to Crusher.

"Ooooh!" Crusher grinned. "Mr Carter, eh? Do you hear that, lads?" He pointed at the others. "Well, that's Mr Willis, Mr Stone and Mr Bunn. And you can call me Mr Capstick!"

The others fell about laughing. I didn't. I was starting to get worried.

"Crusher Capstick?" Dad repeated. "I know that name." He turned to me. "Robbie, is this the boy who's always in trouble at school? Is he a friend of yours?"

I was stuck. I didn't want Dad to know I'd been hanging around with Crusher's gang.

"Yeah, I am," said Crusher. He put his arm round my shoulders. "Robbie's in our gang. Aren't you, Rob?"

"Sort of," I muttered. I couldn't look at Dad.

"I think you and I had better have a little chat, Robbie," Dad said very sternly. "I don't want you getting into trouble, too."

Crusher and the others almost split their sides laughing.

"Listen to him!" Crusher chuckled. "Who does he think he is? He sounds like your dad!"

Dad glared at him. "I don't want any cheek from you, thank you."

Crusher stopped laughing and looked annoyed. I groaned. Why couldn't Dad remember that he was 11 years old?

"Hey, Rob." Crusher slapped me on the back. "You don't want to hang around with this weirdo, do you? We're on our way to the old factory. Why don't you come with us?"

"Yeah, why don't you come with us?" said Ed, Rocky and Kirk together. I opened my mouth to say something. But Dad got in first.

"The old factory?" he said with a frown. "Robbie's not allowed to play there. It's much too dangerous."

Crusher looked at me with a glint in his eye. "Are you going to listen to this bossy little twit, or are you going to come with us?" he asked.

"Robbie's staying right here," Dad said loudly.

I made up my mind. "I'm coming," I said.

Chapter 5
Trouble

"Robbie, I said no!" Dad shouted at me, as I walked off with Crusher and his gang. "Come back here!"

But there wasn't anything he could do. I mean, he was only 11! I kept on walking.

"Let's run for it," Crusher yelled. "Then we can leave that boring little geek behind."

We ran off down the street. When we reached the corner, I looked back. Dad was running after us, but he was a long way behind. He wasn't as fit as he used to be. He used to play football a lot when he was younger. He'd even had a trial at Chelsea FC when he was a kid. But I could see he was already out of breath.

I felt a bit guilty. I knew I shouldn't have run off. But Dad was really getting on my nerves with all that nagging. I was going to enjoy myself for a change.

"That's got rid of *him*!" Crusher laughed. By the time we got to the next corner, we'd left Dad far behind. "Come on, Robbie. The factory's just down here."

The old factory stood behind the High Street. It was a tall, dark building with lots of windows which were all boarded up. The doors were boarded up, too. It looked quite scary.

"How do we get in?" I asked.

Crusher winked at me. "Let's go round the back," he said.

One of the boards on a window at the back of the factory was loose. We pulled it to one side and climbed through.

It was cold and damp inside the factory, and the floor was covered with rubbish. There were skylights in the roof which let in some light, but it was still a bit dark. It was dead spooky. I didn't like it at all, but I tried not to show it.

"I wonder if that stupid mate of yours will follow us," Crusher said, kicking an empty cola can across the floor.

"He's not stupid," I said quickly. Then I wished I'd kept my mouth shut as Crusher turned on me.

"OK." Crusher folded his arms. "I wonder if that *weird* mate of yours will follow us."

"He's not weird," I mumbled. I knew it would be better if I kept quiet. But I didn't like hearing Crusher talk about my dad like that.

"You know what?" Crusher's voice was very calm, but it sent shivers up and down my spine. "You're really starting to get on my nerves."

"Yeah," said Ed, Rocky and Kirk sternly. "You're really starting to get on our nerves."

Crusher jabbed me in the chest with his finger. It hurt. "I reckon you're just as weird as your stupid mate," he went on. "So it's up to you to prove that you're not."

"How?" I asked, trying to look brave.

Crusher smiled a shark-like smile. "Well," he said, "how about you climb up to the top floor?" He pointed up over our heads. "That will show us you're not a boring geek, too."

I frowned. That sounded easy. Too easy. I looked around and saw that all the staircases were boarded up.

"I can't," I said. "There's no way up."

"Oh, yes, there is," Crusher replied with a grin. He pointed at a cracked and battered drainpipe in the corner of the factory which went right up to the roof. Ed, Rocky and Kirk sniggered.

I stared at the drainpipe. It was hanging off the wall in places. I was sure it would snap if I tried to climb it. And when I got up to the top floor, it might not be safe to walk around. I could have a really bad accident.

Whatever Crusher said, there was no way I could do this.

"Go on." Crusher gave me a push. "All you've got to do is climb up that drainpipe."

"Robbie! Don't do it!" called a voice I knew very well.

Dad was climbing in through the window. I groaned to myself. Now things were going to get even more tricky.

"Robbie!" Dad rushed over to us. His face was red and his hair was sticking up all over the place. "What do you think you're doing? I can't believe you'd be so stupid!"

"I wasn't going to—" I began.

"You're coming home with me right now," Dad went on. He wasn't listening to a word I said. He didn't trust me. So what's new?

I'd never felt so cross in my life. I'd had enough.

So I did something I'd wanted to do all day. I flew at Dad, and knocked him over onto the dusty floor.

Then I jumped on top of him, and we began to fight.

Chapter 6
The Fight

Crusher and his gang cheered loudly.

"Fight! Fight!" they yelled, crowding round as Dad and I rolled across the factory floor.

Dad was a useless fighter. He was worse than I was. We both struggled and pushed and pulled and tugged, but neither of us could get a punch in. We were locked together like two boxers in a ring.

I grabbed Dad's T-shirt, he grabbed the leg of my jeans and we started to punch each other. As we did so, I saw the look in Dad's eye.

What on earth was I *doing*?

I was fighting with my 11-year-old dad! This was crazy!

I let go of Dad's T-shirt, and burst out laughing. I couldn't stop myself. Dad blinked at me. Then a grin spread across his face. He began to laugh, too.

"What's so funny?" Crusher asked, looking puzzled. But we were laughing too hard to reply. We were bent over, laughing.

"I want to know what's going on!" Crusher said crossly. Dad and I didn't reply. We held onto each other and almost cried with laughter.

"Right, that's it!" Crusher yelled as we wiped the tears from our eyes. "Unless you tell me what's going on, you're dead!"

"Now, you listen to me," Dad said sternly. He walked forward and stared Crusher in the face. "It's about time you stopped being such a bully. I'm going to have a word with your parents, young man."

Crusher turned purple in the face. You could almost see steam coming out of his ears.

"Dad, you're 11 years old, remember?" I whispered in his ear. "There's only one way out of this."

"What's that?" asked Dad.

"RUN!" I yelled.

Chapter 7
Football Star

I ran off across the factory, dragging Dad with me.

"Get 'em!" Crusher shouted.

We dived out of the window and ran for it. Behind us we could hear Crusher and his gang yelling at each other as they all tried to climb out of the window at the same time.

Dad and I dashed down the road. There was a skip on the corner which was half full with rubbish. Dad grabbed my arm and pulled me behind it. He put his finger to his lips.

We stood there and waited. About half a minute later we heard footsteps.

"Come on!" Crusher shouted. "They can't be far away. That Robbie is so dead when I get my hands on him!"

We heard them rush past us. Then there was silence.

Dad peered out from behind the skip. "They've gone," he said with a grin. "They didn't even think of looking behind the skip!"

I smiled back at him. "Crusher's a bit thick," I replied. Crusher *was* stupid. I don't know why I ever thought he was cool.

"It just goes to show," Dad said, "that brains can beat a bully every time!"

"Yeah," I muttered, "until I go to school on Monday. Crusher's going to be waiting for me."

Dad frowned. "I forgot about that," he said. "Don't worry, Robbie. We'll sort something out."

"Thanks, Dad," I said. "Now, hadn't we better get to the hospital?"

"Yes, you're right," Dad agreed. "Let's take the short cut through the park."

We set off again. Somehow the whole thing with Crusher had made Dad and me feel better about each other. It still wasn't like it used to be. But it was a start.

"I wasn't going to climb up that drainpipe, you know," I said, as we walked through the park.

Dad looked a bit embarrassed. "I know, son," he replied. "I was just worried, that's all. I do trust you."

"Thanks," I said.

A gang of boys were playing football in the park. I stopped when I saw who they were. There was Sam, Ben, Tom, Leroy and Darren, who were all in my class at school. My mate Joe was standing at the ice-cream stall, buying a cone.

"Hi," I said, feeling my face turn red. I wondered if Joe would speak to me. After all, I'd been pretty horrible to him before.

"Hey, Robbie," said Joe with a smile. He looked at Dad. "Who's this?"

"This is my mate, Terry," I explained.

Joe frowned. "Have we met before?" he asked. "You look kind of like someone I know."

Dad and I grinned at each other.

"Do you two want to play football with us?" Joe went on. "We need a few more people."

I thought Dad would say no. But he smiled and nodded.

"Well, maybe just for five minutes," he said. "Come on, Robbie."

We ran across the grass to join the others. Sam, Ben, Tom, Leroy and Darren looked really pleased to see us. I'd been feeling so fed up, I'd forgotten I had so many good mates.

We started playing. Dad and I were on the same team, and Dad was brilliant. He couldn't run very fast because he wasn't very fit, but he could do loads of tricks. He slid the ball through Darren's legs, and passed to me. I hit the ball hard, and it flew past Ben. Goal!

"Your mate's fantastic!" said Joe, as he slapped me on the back. "I wish he came to our school. He could be in our team!"

I smiled. But then I spotted Crusher Capstick and his gang marching towards us. That wiped the smile off my face.

"Oi!" Crusher shouted angrily. "Get over here now, Robbie! You *and* that stupid mate of yours!"

I stayed where I was. Dad, Joe, Ben, Tom, Sam, Darren and Leroy came and stood next to me.

"What do you want, Crusher?" I asked.

"You're not in my gang any more, you wimp!" Crusher sneered.

"Good," I said. "Anything else?"

Crusher curled his hands into fists. But then he looked round at me and all my mates. He only had Ed, Rocky and Kirk to back him up.

"No," Crusher mumbled. "Just keep out of my way from now on!" he said as he turned to go.

"Don't worry," I replied. "I will."

We all laughed as Crusher and his gang hurried off.

"I don't think you'll have any more trouble from him!" said Dad. "Now, what about this game?"

We carried on playing. Dad scored two goals, and we won three-one. Then we had to go. We'd been there much longer than five minutes!

"Bye, Joe," I called. "See you at school on Monday."

"OK." Joe waved at me. "Listen, my dad's joining a new football team at the sports centre. He told me to ask your dad to join, too."

I glanced at Dad. "I'll tell him," I replied.

"Are you getting on better with him now?" Joe asked.

I laughed. "Yeah, much better!"

Dad and I walked off across the park.

"You should join that football team," I said.

"I will," said Dad. "I'd forgotten how much I enjoyed playing." He coughed. "Look, Robbie, I know things haven't been easy since your mum left. But I'm going to try harder from now on."

"Me, too," I agreed. "I just wish we could get on this well when you go back to being Dad again!"

Chapter 8
Dad's Grown Up!

Suddenly I felt a little dizzy. I blinked and shook my head to clear it.

Dad was standing in front of me. It *was* Dad! He was 32 years old again. He looked normal, except that his jeans and T-shirt were much too small for him!

"I'm all right again!" Dad gasped. He stared down at himself in amazement. "Thank goodness."

"Do you feel OK?" I asked.

Dad nodded. "I feel fine."

"You look like you're about to burst out of those clothes!" I laughed. People walking past us were giving Dad some very funny looks. "Come on, let's go home."

We hurried home. While Dad got changed, I went into my bedroom and put my computer on. But that weird junk e-mail had vanished from the screen.

Dad came in as I turned my computer off. "I still don't understand what happened," he said, looking puzzled. "Still, I'm back to normal now. That's all that matters." He grinned at me. "Shall we watch a video tonight, and order a pizza?"

"Great!" I beamed. "We haven't done that for ages."

"Things are going to be different now," Dad replied.

We were waiting for the pizza to arrive when the doorbell rang. I opened the door, thinking it would be the pizza man. It wasn't. It was Joe.

"Hi," he said. "You left your jacket at the park, Robbie." And he handed it over.

"Why don't you stay, Joe?" Dad said, coming out of the kitchen. "We're having pizza."

"Great!" Joe agreed happily. He came in and I shut the door. "Where's your mate, Terry?"

I glanced at Dad. "Oh, he's around somewhere," I replied. And we both burst out laughing.

Barrington Stoke would like to thank all its readers for commenting on the manuscript before publication and in particular:

Harriet Aish

Christine Bilham

Christopher Chester-Sterne

Sean Cragg

James Darling

Lewis Judd

Sam Kouzarides

David Morgan

Trudy Morgan

Lucy Robinson

Michael Runham

Max Thompson

Chloe Upton

Charlotte Wetherell

Become a Consultant!

Would you like to give us feedback on our titles before they are published? Contact us at the address below – we'd love to hear from you!

Barrington Stoke, Sandeman House, Trunk's Close,
55 High Street, Edinburgh EH1 1SR
Tel: 0131 557 2020 Fax: 0131 557 6060
E-mail: info@barringtonstoke.co.uk
Website: www.barringtonstoke.co.uk

If you loved this story, why don't you read . . .

Best in the World
by Chris Powling
ISBN 1-842992-05-8
£4.99

Have you ever wanted to push yourself to the limit? Lucas and Jeb are ready to do the "Triple" and become the best trapeze artists in the world. But will they risk their lives to follow a dream?

You can order *Best in the World* directly from our website at www.barringtonstoke.co.uk

If you loved this story, why don't you read . . .

Weird Happenings

by Kaye Umansky

ISBN 1-842992-07-4

£4.99

Have you ever wanted to stay at home when your parents go off to visit family? That's what Pinchton Primm did. But when he invites the Weird family from next door round to his house, things start to go horribly wrong. Will he ever get everything back to normal *before* his parents get home?

You can order *Weird Happenings* directly from our website at www.barringtonstoke.co.uk

If you loved this story, why don't you read . . .

Game Boy

by Alan Durant

ISBN 1-842991-17-5

£4.99

Have you got a GameBoy? J P loves his GameBoy and he can't wait to try out his new game. But, as it starts, a strange message appears. J P finds himself in a thrilling life and death adventure and there's no going back. Will he make the right choices? Can he get past the dangers? Is he good enough to make it to the end of the game?

You can order _Game Boy_ directly from our website at www.barringtonstoke.co.uk